Fairy in Danger

Twink

Bimi

Pix

Sooze

Sili

Mariella

Kiki

Ivy

Book Fourteen

Fairy in Danger

Titania Woods
Illustrated by Smiljana Coh

BLOOMSBURY

LONDON BERLIN NEW YORK

Bloomsbury Publishing, London, Berlin and New York

First published in Great Britain in July 2010 by Bloomsbury Publishing Plc
36 Soho Square, London, W1D 3QY

A CIP catalogue record of this book is available from the British Library

ISBN 978 1 4088 0268 7

All papers used by Bloomsbury Publishing are natural, recyclable products made
from wood grown in well-managed forests. The manufacturing processes conform to
the environmental regulations of the country of origin.

Typeset by Dorchester Typesetting Group Ltd
Printed in Singapore by Tien Wah Press

1 3 5 7 9 10 8 6 4 2

www.glitterwingsacademy.co.uk

To the Fairy Protection Squad,
with love and thanks

Chapter One

Hurrah, we're back at Glitterwings Academy! Twink Flutterby smiled as she and her little sister Teena landed on the green, grassy lawn.

The giant oak tree that housed their school towered above them. The grand double doors at its base stood open, and arched windows spiralled up its trunk, sparkling brightly in the sunshine. Everywhere Twink looked, there were returning fairies. They swooped about calling to each other, or flew in and out of the school in a busy stream.

Twink sighed contentedly as she put down her

oak-leaf bag. 'Glitterwings is *so* pretty in the summertime,' she said.

Teena laughed. 'You sound just like Mum!'

Twink grinned as she realised her little sister was right. Their mother had also gone to Glitterwings as a young fairy, and was always exclaiming over its beauty in every season.

'Well, it *is*, though,' insisted Twink. 'Look how green its leaves are!'

'You look – I'm going to go and find Zuzu,' said Teena, referring to her best friend. 'See you later, Twink!' She sped off towards the second-year section, her long pink hair and lavender wings looking very like Twink's own.

Twink stood where she was for a moment, still gazing upwards. Suddenly her violet eyes widened. What was *that*? There had been a flash of light at the top of the school, like a wink of fire!

Wings fluttering, Twink lifted up from the ground. She could just make out a slender branch growing right at the tree's peak. The light she'd seen was a window, catching the sun.

2

Twink stared at it in surprise. She'd been going to Glitterwings for over three years now, and she'd never known that there were any branches with windows that high up! What was the little branch used for?

'Twink!' cried a voice. With a flurry of gold and silver wings, her best friend Bimi Bluebell came fluttering up, skimming over the grass.

Twink forgot all about the strange branch as she and Bimi hugged. 'It's so good to see you!' she cried.

'I know, it's been ages,' said Bimi happily. 'Come on, let's go and check in with Miss Petal. Then we

can fly up to Bluebell Branch and grab our beds.' Their branch this year had the same name as Bimi's surname, which caused a lot of good-natured teasing for her!

Soon the two friends were swooping through the double doors into their school. Glitterwings rose above them like a tall, golden tower. Fairies fluttered in and out of its branches for as high as the eye could see.

Twink and Bimi flew upwards, passing sleeping branches and empty classrooms. Remembering the funny little branch she'd seen, Twink described it to Bimi. 'Isn't that strange?' she said when she'd finished. 'What do you think is up there?'

Bimi shook her head. 'I don't think there *are* any branches with windows that high up,' she said, banking to avoid a cluster of second-year students. 'Are you sure, Twink? Maybe the sun was in your eyes.'

'Maybe,' said Twink doubtfully. She had certainly *thought* she'd seen a window, but she supposed she could have been wrong. It seemed very odd, though.

The two fairies landed on the ledge of Bluebell Branch. Pushing open the door, Twink smiled to see their familiar home. Bluebell Branch was like a little tower, growing straight up and down with two loft spaces encircling its walls. A bright cluster of blue-bells dangled from its ceiling, like a chandelier made of flowers.

Some of the other fairies had already arrived, and a chorus of hellos greeted them. 'Opposite! You and Bimi can join us up here; we've got two beds left!' called a voice from the upper loft. Glancing up, Twink saw Sooze and Sili waving at them.

Twink and Bimi grinned at each other. It would be lovely to have beds on the top level for a change – and without the snooty Mariella, who had been up there last term!

They fluttered quickly upwards. Sooze flung herself at Twink in a hug. 'Hello, Opposite!' she said cheerfully. It had been her nickname for Twink since their very first term together, because her lavender hair and pink wings were the exact *opposite* of Twink's.

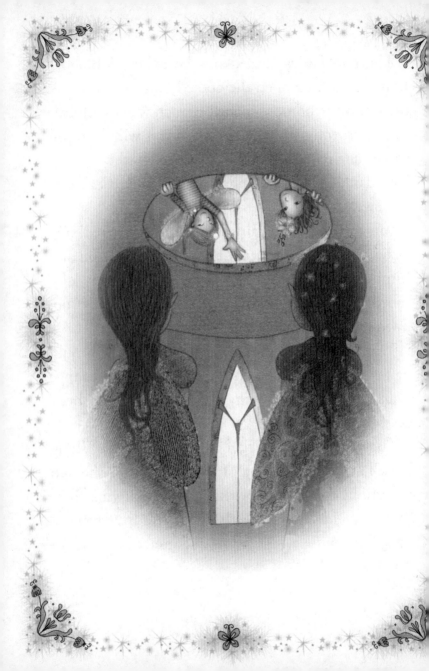

'Hi, Sooze!' said Twink, returning the hug.

'Isn't it glimmery up here?' said Sili, bouncing on her bed. She was an excitable fairy with silver hair and a breathless way of talking. 'I bet we have loads of fun this term!'

Bimi and Twink took two beds side by side, with a large window between them. Placing her favourite drawing of her family on her bedside mushroom, Twink looked around her with a contented sigh. Pretty clusters of bluebells hung over their mossy beds, and a soft carpet of lighter moss lay underfoot. Oh, it was lovely to be back!

'I can hardly wait for tomorrow,' said Sooze. 'I've got a great idea for my bluebell dress!' Putting a hand behind her head, she waggled her hips with a grin.

Twink and Bimi laughed. Fourth-year fairies were allowed to make their own flower uniforms with fairy dust – and last term Sooze had horrified Mrs Hover, the matron, with a flouncy skirt and feathery boa! 'What is it this time?' asked Twink eagerly.

But Sooze shook her head. 'It's a secret – you'll just have to wait and see!'

Once everyone had unpacked, it was time for the opening session in the Great Branch. The breeze rustled through Twink's lavender wings as she glided with the other Bluebell fairies down the trunk, joining long lines of fairies from other branches and year groups.

The Great Branch was the largest branch in the school. It had shining wooden floors and was filled with long rows of mossy tables, each with a different flower hanging over it. Sunlight dazzled through its windows, making the Branch look like a glorious garden.

Twink folded her wings behind her back as she and her friends settled at the Bluebell table. She spotted Teena sitting with the Daisy Branch fairies, and the two sisters exchanged a friendly smile.

Once all the students had gathered, Miss Shimmery took to the air at the front of the Branch, hovering above them. 'Welcome back!' she said in her low voice. Her rainbow wings gleamed in the sunlight. 'I've just a few announcements . . .'

As the HeadFairy gave her usual talk, Twink gazed out of the window, wondering again about the strange branch she'd seen. Despite what Bimi had said, she didn't think she'd been mistaken. What could the little branch be used for, so high up? It would be much too small for a classroom or dorm.

Suddenly Twink's pointed ears perked up as Miss Shimmery said, 'Finally, we're going to do a special project this term. I'd like each student to find out something about Glitterwings that she never knew before, and write a report on it. The most interesting reports in each year will win prizes.'

A special project – how glimmery! The Branch erupted into excited murmurs. With a smile, Miss Shimmery raised her arms. 'Now then, I think it's time to eat. Butterflies commence!'

As the HeadFairy drifted back down to the platform, the doors to the Great Branch swung open. A bright stream of butterflies floated in, each carrying a tray of seed cakes or an acorn pitcher of fresh dew.

The Bluebell Branch fairies burst into conversation. 'The project sounds like fun, doesn't it?' said Ivy. She had light green curly hair, and was very artistic.

Kiki, her best friend, nodded. 'I think I'll research what sort of uniforms the students wore when Glitterwings was first founded,' she said.

'Ooh, yes!' said Ivy. 'We could even make models of them!'

Mariella sniffed. 'Well, *I* think we have enough on at the moment, without doing special projects, too,' she said, flipping back her silvery-green hair. 'After all, we've got our Sapling Exams coming up this year. It's not very considerate of Miss Shimmery to –'

'Oh hush, Mosquito Nose,' said Sooze cheerfully. She helped herself to a seed cake. 'It won't hurt you to stretch your brain a bit. Who knows, it might enjoy the exercise!'

Pix, the cleverest fairy in their branch, tapped her yellow wings together. 'There must be *loads* that nobody knows about Glitterwings,' she mused. 'It's such a large school, and so old! I'll have to go to the library tomorrow and do some research.' Her eyes sparkled at the thought.

Sili shook her head. 'Pix, it's not supposed to be something that *nobody* knows about Glitterwings – just something that *you* don't know.'

Pix looked surprised. 'What's the fun of that? I want to have the best report of all!'

'We'll see about that,' sang Ivy with a pointed smile. Pix pulled a face at her, and everyone laughed. The clever fairy loved earning the highest marks in their year, and often did – unless Ivy's twin sister Jade beat her!

Bimi leaned her head close to Twink's. 'You should do a report on your mystery branch,' she whispered. 'If it really exists, that is.'

Twink smiled as she drizzled honey over her seed cake . . . and then thought that, actually, that wasn't a bad idea at all!

The next morning a pile of fresh bluebell blossoms was left on the Bluebell Branch ledge by one of the school birds. Kiki brought them in with a smile.

'Flowers, everyone!' she called.

Still wearing her dandelion-fluff dressing gown, Twink fluttered down to the main level with the others. 'Ooh, these are pretty ones,' said Bimi, picking up a blossom. 'Look, Twink, here's a nice dark one to go with my hair.'

'Glimmery!' said Twink, choosing one of her own. Taking a bit of fairy dust from the pouch at her hip, she thought for a moment, imagining the dress she wanted. Then she sprinkled it over the flower in a flurry of pink and gold.

Pfff! The blossom changed into a pretty blue dress with short, tight sleeves, a plain bodice, and a skirt made of tiny bluebell flowers.

Twink changed into her new outfit, admiring herself in the mirror that hung on the wall. She was *so* glad to be a Fourth Year, and able to make her own dress each term. It was much more satisfying than having Mrs Hover do it for her!

All around Twink, there were similar flashes of pink and gold as the other fairies made their uniforms, too. 'What do you think?' said Bimi, pressing next to Twink in the mirror. Her dress was very like Twink's, except that the sleeves were a bit longer.

'Lovely!' Twink assured her. 'It really suits –' She broke off as Sooze's voice echoed loudly through the branch.

'Ta-daaa!' cried the lavender-haired fairy, drifting down from the top level with her arms out. 'What do you think of my creation, everyone?' Landing, she struck a pose with a flourish.

'*Sooze!*' squealed Mariella. 'You can't wear *that*!'

'Why not?' said Sooze innocently, as the rest of

the branch howled with laughter. 'Don't you like it?'

'It's very *you*, Sooze,' said Pix finally, between guffaws.

Giggling helplessly, Twink thought that that was a very tactful way of putting it! Sooze's new outfit had a bikini top, and a bluebell skirt that was short at the front and long at the back. Around her head was a headband with a long feather in it, and there were frilly armbands just above each elbow.

'Well, *I* think it's glimmery,' said Sooze. She tottered over to the mirror on high heels, with her skirt swishing behind her. 'Look, everyone, it's even got sequins!'

'Not for long, it hasn't,' said Mrs Hover grimly. The Bluebell Branch fairies jumped. None of them had noticed the matron's arrival, but now she stood just inside their doorway, shaking her head.

'Honestly, I have to watch you like a cat,' she scolded Sooze, fluttering over and snatching the headband off her head. 'Now, go and change that horror into a proper dress!'

'Oh, Hovey, can't I just wear it to breakfast?'

pleaded Sooze. 'Please? I'd love to see everyone's faces!'

'Away with you, you shameless thing,' ordered Mrs Hover, giving Sooze a light push between her wings. She shook her head with a smile as Sooze flapped off to the top level again.

'Right, I've got your timetables, my dears,' she announced, holding up a sheaf of rose petals. The fairies crowded around her as she passed them out.

Twink scanned the pink petal with her name on it eagerly. Star Magic II, Advanced Creature Kindness II, Advanced Flower Power II . . . her classes were just the same as last term. And, as she'd hoped, she had a free hour after her Advanced Creature Kindness lesson.

That's when I'll go looking for the little branch, decided Twink. Her wings tingled with excitement at the thought. What would she find up there?

Chapter Two

Twink's lessons that day seemed to drag past, until finally it was time for Creature Kindness. Though this was usually Twink's favourite class, today she could hardly wait for it to be over, so that she could begin looking for the strange branch.

'Now, ah . . . when dealing with larger mammals, it's essential to, ah . . . gain their trust,' mumbled Mr Woodleaf.

Twink held back a smile. As usual, Mr Woodleaf seemed terrified of his students!

He cleared his throat. 'I'll just, ah . . . get a

patient, and show you what I mean.'

The girls glanced at each other curiously as Mr Woodleaf flitted off behind the Creature Kindness log. Twink had been as surprised as the others to learn that their Creature Kindness lesson was taking place outside that day – but she suddenly understood why when Mr Woodleaf reappeared from behind the log, leading a badger!

A startled gasp ran through the class. Badgers had a reputation for being fierce. They were certainly large – this one was easily ten times the size of a fairy. The black and grey creature glared at them with red-rimmed eyes.

Twink swallowed uneasily . . . and then felt a pang of sympathy as she saw that the badger had an injured paw. The poor thing! No wonder it was cross.

'You see, he's quite nervous,' said Mr Woodleaf, reaching up and stroking the badger's grey neck. 'So before we can help him, we need to, ah . . . calm him down. Does anyone know how?'

Pix raised her hand. 'Shall we sing to him?' she

suggested. Several girls nodded in agreement. Fairy song was magical, and many creatures found it soothing. It was used for healing sometimes, too.

But Mr Woodleaf shook his head. 'No, badgers hate singing, I'm afraid! Think, girls . . . what do badgers like best of all?'

Twink's pink eyebrows drew together as she tried to recall everything that she knew about the striped mammals. They usually came out at night . . . they liked to eat all different sorts of things . . .

Suddenly Bimi's hand flew up. 'I know!' she cried, fluttering her wings. 'They like being in their setts, don't they?'

Mr Woodleaf beamed, and seemed to forget his nervousness. 'Exactly!' he cried. 'Badgers love being in their underground homes, which are called *setts*. Well done, Bimi.'

Twink felt a rush of pride as she and Bimi smiled at each other. Her best friend had worked very hard to get into this advanced class, and now she did just as well as any of them.

'So to calm him down, we need to make him

think that that's exactly where he is,' continued Mr Woodleaf, patting the badger's chest. 'Who's good at casting glamours?'

Glamours were a special kind of spell that made you see things that weren't really there. 'That would be you, Mosquito Nose!' said Sooze, nudging the pointy-faced fairy with a grin.

Mariella's cheeks turned pink with pleasure as she stepped forward. It was true, thought Twink. Though lazy at most of her studies, Mariella was brilliant at Star Magic, the art of illusion. She could cast the most convincing glamours of any of them!

Murmuring to herself and moving her hands about, Mariella quickly cast the spell. All at once everything went dark as the sunny glade seemed to turn into a snug underground hole. Peering around her, Twink's eyes widened in admiration. Mariella had even thought to put roots in place, and the rich scent of the earth!

Though all of the fairies could see through the glamour, the badger blinked in surprise to find

himself suddenly transported underground. Sniffing deeply at the clammy air, he stretched out on the ground with a happy sigh.

'Good work!' said Mr Woodleaf. 'Now we can tend to his paw.'

By the end of the lesson the badger was snoozing peacefully, his hurt paw neatly bandaged. Twink smiled in satisfaction as she and the other students fluttered back to school.

'Are you going to try and find your mystery branch now?' asked Bimi.

Twink nodded. 'Definitely!' She looked towards the top of the tree, trying to remember exactly where she had seen the strange branch. But though she saw lots of leaves, and even a bird's nest or two, she couldn't spot the little window.

'Well, I don't think it's there, but good luck anyway,' laughed Bimi as they swooped into the school. 'If you don't find it, then come and join me in the library.'

'All right,' agreed Twink, adjusting her petal bag over her shoulder. 'But you'll see, Bimi – there *is* something up there, I just know it!'

Saying goodbye, she took off, spiralling further and further up the tree. The number of fairies dwindled, until at last she was the only one flying so high. She felt a thrill of excitement as she passed the entrance to the star-gazing platform. This was as far up the tree as she'd ever gone!

She continued upwards. Soon the walls of the trunk began to narrow around her, and the air felt stale and dusty. Clearly, no one had ventured so high in ages.

Finally the trunk became so slender that Twink could hardly stretch her wings to fly. Hovering awkwardly, she sighed in disappointment. Bimi must have been right after all – there *couldn't* be a branch used by fairies up here!

But then Twink looked up, and caught her breath. Starting just above her head were a series of tiny knotholes going up the trunk – almost like those things humans called stairs! Quickly folding her wings behind her back, she grabbed hold of them and began to climb.

The narrow passageway took her higher and higher, twisting and turning. Just when Twink was beginning to wonder whether it was a dead end after all, she came to a dim, dusty ledge. She pulled herself on to it . . . and her heartbeat quickened.

There, in the shadowy light, she could just make out a door! It was barely as tall as she was, with an arched top and wooden grooves that were thick with dust.

Twink gazed down at its handle, feeling oddly shy.

It didn't seem right to just go barging in. Besides . . . what if *someone* was already inside? Her wings went clammy at the thought.

Raising her hand, she knocked softly. 'Hello?' she called.

Silence. Twink smiled in relief. Of course there wasn't anyone in there – it was probably just an old storage branch! Shaking her head at herself, she reached for the handle and pushed.

There was a faint *click* . . . and the door swung open.

Twink stepped inside, ducking slightly. The ceiling was so low that she could hardly stand up straight! Her eyes widened as she took in the little room.

There was a single round window, through which sunlight shone. A small, plain bed stood against one wall. In the centre of the narrow branch was a rickety-looking table and chair, and up on a shelf there were rows and rows of . . . things.

Twink stared. What *were* they? Each item was smooth and white, about the size of her hand, but

carved in the most amazing patterns! There was an owl, and a frog, and something that looked like a bat. Moving forward, Twink picked up the bat for a closer look.

'What are you doing?' demanded an angry voice. 'Put that down!'

Stifling a shriek, Twink whirled round.

The window was now open, and crouching on the sill, as if she had just landed, was a fairy. But she was like no fairy Twink had ever seen. She was tiny, with untidy jet-black hair and silvery-grey wings – and she looked absolutely furious.

'I'm – I'm sorry,' stammered Twink. Hastily, she put the carving back on the shelf. 'I just –'

'You just *what*?' Hopping into the room, the fairy banged the window shut behind her. She was wearing a grey and black dress, and stockings with black and white stripes. Though she looked about Twink's age, she was at least a head shorter.

'I was just exploring,' said Twink, trying not to stare. 'You see, I saw this branch from outside the school, and –'

'And so you thought you'd come up here and snoop about!' The black-haired fairy strode over to the shelf, taking the bat down and inspecting it carefully. She glared at Twink. 'How dare you come in here and touch my private things?'

Twink felt a flash of anger. 'I said I was sorry! I didn't know that someone *lived* here. Anyway, who are you? You're not one of the students here.'

'No, I'm not one of the students – as if I would be!' The fairy gave a disgusted shudder, and carefully put the bat back in place beside the other carvings.

'All right, but who *are* you?' pressed Twink. 'My name's Twink,' she added, to be polite.

At first she thought the other fairy wasn't going to answer, but then she shrugged sulkily. 'I'm called Shadow,' she said. 'And as to what I'm doing here . . . well, why not? No one seemed to be using this branch. I haven't done any harm.'

Glancing around, Twink had to agree – the room was neat and tidy, and looked well cared for. 'But what are you doing here?' she pressed. 'You're about

my age, aren't you? Don't you go to school?'

'Are you always this nosy?' said Shadow, folding her arms across her chest. 'No, I don't go to school. I'm far too busy for that – we all are!'

Twink blinked in confusion. Surely the little branch was too small for more than one fairy? 'Who's we?' she asked.

'All of us,' said Shadow. 'I'm not the only one of my kind, you know – just the only one who lives *here*.'

'You mean . . . you're a different sort of fairy than I am?' stammered Twink. Now that Shadow had

said it, it seemed obvious. Twink had never seen a fairy so small before, or with such black hair and pale skin.

Shadow heaved a sigh, rolling her eyes. 'Yes, of course!' She swept an arm at the shelf. 'What do you think *those* are?'

'Carvings,' said Twink, puzzled.

'Yes, but what are they made of?' said Shadow impatiently. When Twink shook her head, she snatched up the owl. 'Look! It's hard, it's white . . .'

Twink gasped in sudden understanding. 'It's a *tooth*,' she breathed in amazement. She could see now that the other carvings were teeth as well. Rows and rows of them, all carved into different designs!

'Brilliant!' said Shadow. 'Yes, that's it. I'm a tooth fairy.'

'You mean – one of those fairies who collect human teeth?' squeaked Twink. 'But I didn't think they actually existed!'

Shadow looked ready to explode with rage. She plonked the owl back on the shelf. 'Oh, typical! *You* lot only know about woods and nature, don't you?

Well, we exist, all right! And we perform a very useful service, too. What would humans do with their old teeth, if it weren't for us?'

'I . . . don't know,' said Twink, her thoughts spinning. Having lived with a human family once, she had been surprised to find that humans *did* have magic, though of a very different sort than her own. Perhaps tooth fairies were a part of this magic, too.

'Well, exactly,' said Shadow, seeming a bit soothed. 'Anyway, you've had your snoop now, so you can leave.'

'Oh,' said Twink. There were still so many questions that she wanted to ask! But Shadow had taken her by the elbow, and was walking her firmly to the door.

'Wait a minute,' said Twink. 'Could you tell me why –'

'Goodbye,' interrupted Shadow, shoving her out on to the ledge. Twink blinked in surprise as the door banged shut in her face.

Chapter
Three

'Hey!' called Twink, leaning against the door. 'Do you think I could come back sometime?'

'What would you want to do *that* for?' replied Shadow's muffled voice. 'Go away!'

Twink hesitated for a moment, and then decided that she'd better do as Shadow asked. Slowly, she made her way back down the knothole ladder, and was soon gliding through the main part of the trunk.

She shook her head in amazement as she flew past a cluster of chatting Third Years. Who would ever have imagined that tooth fairies were real – and that

one of them lived at Glitterwings Academy!

It would make an amazing report for her project
. . . but of course she couldn't write about it, realised
Twink. It wouldn't be fair to give Shadow away
when she wasn't doing any harm. Still, it was a
shame. She'd have been certain to win a prize with
such an original report!

As Twink flitted into the library she spotted Bimi
and Sooze hovering high overhead, looking at a
book on one of the shelves near the ceiling. She flew
up to join them.

Bimi burst into giggles when she saw her. 'Twink!
What have you been doing? You're as dirty as an
earthworm!'

Glancing down at herself, Twink saw that Bimi
was right. Her bluebell dress was covered with
smudges of dust from wriggling her way through
the narrow passage.

Sooze reached out and plucked a cobweb from
Twink's hair. 'Very attractive,' she laughed, dangling
it in front of her. 'Where have you been, anyway?'

Taking a thistle comb from her petal bag, Twink

quickly pulled it through her long pink hair. 'Just wait until I tell you,' she said as she tucked the comb away again. 'And listen, you two – you're never going to believe it!'

'I don't believe it,' said Sooze flatly. 'A *tooth* fairy? She was having you on, Twink.'

'Sooze! She was not!' protested Twink. The three of them were sitting at one of the mushroom tables in the corner of the library, with their wings spread for privacy.

'It does sound a bit funny, Twink, you have to

admit,' said Bimi. 'If she's really a tooth fairy, then what's she doing here at Glitterwings?'

'I don't know,' admitted Twink. 'She, um . . . threw me out before I could ask.'

Bimi and Sooze glanced at each other, their eyebrows raised doubtfully. Twink felt a twinge of irritation. Though it was lovely that her two favourite fairies got along now, it wasn't fair that neither of them believed her!

'What were her carvings, then, if they weren't teeth?' she demanded.

Sooze lifted her wing. 'How should I know? Wood, maybe?'

'Or maybe they *were* teeth, but from some sort of animal,' offered Bimi. 'I just can't believe she was really a tooth fairy, Twink! I mean . . . well . . . they don't exist, do they?'

Twink tapped her wings together crossly. If she hadn't seen the little fairy for herself, she knew that she probably wouldn't believe it either – but even so, this was very frustrating!

'Look, I know it sounds mad –' she started.

'Hang on, *I* know what to do,' broke in Sooze, her violet eyes glinting. 'I'm going to fly up there and meet this *tooth fairy* for myself!'

Twink hesitated. On the one wing, she was sure that Shadow wanted to be left alone . . . but on the other, she hadn't actually *forbidden* Twink to come back. And it would be glimmery to show Sooze that she was right!

'We'll both go,' she decided. 'Why don't we sneak up there after glow-worms out tonight?'

'You're on!' said Sooze with a grin. 'Are you coming, Bimi?'

'Up that narrow space?' said Bimi. She shuddered. 'No, thank you!' Bimi had a dread of closed-in places, and had listened with a look of horror as Twink described her journey.

'All right, it's just us, then,' said Sooze. She nudged Twink's wing with her own. 'I can hardly wait to meet this tooth fairy of yours, Opposite! I wonder what she *really* is.'

'She's a tooth fairy,' said Twink firmly. 'Just wait and see!'

The trunk was dark and silent as Twink and Sooze slipped out of their branch that night, still wearing their bluebell dresses. They flew quickly upwards, stifling their giggles.

Twink felt a rush of excitement. It had been a long time since she'd been on an adventure with Sooze! It made her feel like a giddy first-year student again, instead of a mature and sensible Fourth Year.

'Is it above here?' asked Sooze in surprise as they passed the entrance to the star-gazing platform. 'I thought this was practically the top of the tree!'

'I did, too,' said Twink as she led the way up the narrowing trunk, 'but it goes on for quite a bit. It gets really hard to fly in, though, so I suppose no one bothers coming up this high.'

Soon they were clambering up the knothole ladder together, with Twink leading the way. She hopped up on to the dusty ledge. 'There's the door,' she said in a low voice.

Sooze's eyes were shining as she joined her.

'Glimmery! I can't believe we've never come up here before – what a splendid hideout!'

'We're too old for hideouts,' laughed Twink.

'Speak for yourself!' said Sooze. 'Why, I bet –'

'Who's there?' demanded a sharp voice on the other side of the door.

They fell silent. *Is that her?* mouthed Sooze.

Twink nodded, suddenly feeling a bit guilty. She knew that Shadow didn't want any company – perhaps they should just leave her alone.

'Sooze, maybe –' she whispered.

The door swung open. '*You* again,' said Shadow. To Twink's surprise, her eyes were red and puffy. 'Go away! As if I didn't have enough problems, without –' She broke off with a scowl, wiping a hand across her eyes.

Twink and Sooze glanced at each other, all laughter gone. 'What problems?' said Twink. 'Could we help, maybe?'

Shadow snorted. 'Oh, right. Pull the other wing! Why would *you* want to help *me*?'

'Because we're nice, that's why,' said Sooze sharply.

'But if you don't want us to help you, then fine – we'll leave!'

Shadow looked taken aback. She stared at them for a moment, obviously thinking hard. 'Maybe you *can* help,' she said suddenly. Stepping back, she opened the door wider. 'Anyway, come in, and I'll tell you about it.'

Twink and Sooze stepped into the branch. Twink saw her friend's expression turn to wonder as she took in the small furniture and the rows of carvings – not to mention Shadow herself, with her black hair and silvery-grey wings.

'Are you really a tooth fairy?' asked Sooze.

Shadow glared at her. '*Yes*. I suppose now you're going to say that we don't exist, aren't you?'

Sooze looked guilty. 'Er – no,' she said. 'You seem to exist all right!'

'Shadow, what can we help you with?' asked Twink.

The tooth fairy hesitated for a moment, biting her lip. Finally she said, 'Well, you see, I – I've sprained my wing, and now I can't go out on a tooth-collecting mission tonight.'

Twink gazed at Shadow's wing. She was no expert, but it looked fine to her. 'Could we try some healing magic on you?' she suggested. 'Or we could ask if one of the teachers would –'

'No!' cried Shadow. 'I don't want any of your magic. My wing will heal on its own. I just need some help – but I suppose I should have known you didn't really mean it.'

'Oh, I get it,' said Sooze. 'You want one of us to go tooth-collecting for you!'

Shadow nodded eagerly, taking a step forward. '*Would* you? It's only one house, and it's not even that far from here – it wouldn't take any time at all.'

'Well, Twink's the expert on humans, not me,' said Sooze. She glanced at Twink with a grin.

Twink rolled her eyes. 'Shadow, wouldn't it be easier if we just healed your wing? I don't think it can be sprained all that badly –'

'No, I've told you!' insisted Shadow. 'All I need is for one of you to go and collect the tooth for me. It won't take long, I promise.'

'Come on, Opposite, where's your sense of adventure?' Sooze's eyes danced with mischief. 'How often do you get a chance to stand in for a tooth fairy? It'll be brilliant!'

'So why don't *you* do it?' asked Twink, propping her hands on her hips.

'Maybe I will,' said Sooze thoughtfully. 'We've all been getting far too sensible lately. It's been ages since we sneaked out of school – and look what a beautiful night it is!'

Twink looked out of the open window. The moon was a bright, shining silver, and she could feel a

mild breeze ruffling her hair. Excitement tickled across her wings. Sooze was right. It *would* be fun to sneak out and have an adventure.

'All right – I *will* go!' she decided all at once. 'Why not?'

The little tooth fairy breathed a sigh of relief. 'Right, then,' she said, pulling Twink to one side. 'Here's what you need to know . . .'

In no time at all, Twink had slipped through the window and was gliding through the summer night, with Glitterwings Academy growing smaller and smaller behind her. Sparkling stars blanketed the sky.

She banked to avoid a passing moth, and then did a mid-air twirl out of sheer joy. Oh, this was lovely! And she had the pleasure of knowing that she was helping Shadow out, too.

Hanging from her shoulder was a bag that the tooth fairy had given her, which had a coin in it to exchange for the human tooth. The little fairy had scowled when Twink asked her where she'd got it from.

'Fountains,' she'd said shortly. 'Humans throw coins into them to make wishes, you know. So we tooth fairies scoop the coins out, and then swap them for teeth. Easy!'

Privately, Twink thought that it may have been easy, but it wasn't very nice. Still, she supposed that the tooth fairies had to exchange something for the teeth they took – though why they collected them in the first place was a mystery to her!

Following the tooth fairy's directions, Twink soon left the fields and woods behind and came to a street of human houses, dimly lit by street lamps. She hovered high overhead. Shadow had said it was the house on the end, and so it must be that one with the large garden.

Swooping down, Twink circled the house until she found an open window on the first floor, just as Shadow had described. Her heart thumping, Twink landed on the sill and peered into the room.

From the soft glow of a night light, she could see a bed with a sleeping human boy in it. His blond hair was tousled, and Twink smiled, remembering

the human girl she'd once made friends with. Lindsay had had blonde hair, too.

Twink flew into the room. A parade of toys lined the shelves, and there was a lamp shaped like a racing car on the bedside table. Landing beside it, Twink suddenly saw that she'd touched down on a handwritten note. She squinted to make out the faint letters.

Dear Tooth Fairy,
Please would you collect my tooth, which I have left under my pillow for you. Thank you very, very much.
Yours sincerely,
Timmy Hopkins

Twink felt warm as she read it. What a nice, polite boy!

Looking more closely at the sleeping Timmy, she saw that he was wearing blue pyjamas, and cuddling a teddy bear to his chest.

Twink gazed at his pillow, wondering again why

the teeth were left in such an awkward place. It wouldn't be very easy for her to get to it.

'Tradition,' Shadow had said when she'd asked. 'You'll be fine – just crawl under the pillow, grab the tooth, and away you go.' She'd made it sound very simple, but looking now at the large, soft pillow, Twink wasn't so sure. Still, she supposed she had to try.

She flitted over to the bed and touched down beside the pillow. Timmy's sleeping head loomed above her. He snored softly, ruffling her pink hair in the breeze.

The mattress felt spongy under her feet as Twink made her way to the edge of the pillow. *Well – here goes*, she thought. Dropping to her knees, she took a deep breath and crawled underneath it.

Chapter Four

It was worse than being underground! Twink held her breath as she inched along, hating the feeling of the pillow pressing so closely around her. Finally her groping fingers brushed against something cool and smooth.

Twink pulled the coin from her bag and placed it on the sheet. Grabbing hold of the tooth she backed quickly out again, pulling it along with her. She gasped in relief as she came out into the open. She'd done it!

Carefully, Twink tucked the tooth into the bag.

Adjusting the strap so that it lay securely across her chest, she stretched her wings and took off towards the open window.

BOING!

'AAARRGGHHH!' screamed Twink as she hurtled backwards through the air. Struggling to right herself, she shrieked again as she saw that Timmy wasn't asleep after all. He was standing up on his bed, tugging on a thread – and it was attached to her pouch!

The tooth! There had been a thread tied around it to trap her! Twink fumbled wildly with the bag, straining to get rid of it – but it was too late. Timmy had reeled in the last bit of thread, and suddenly Twink found herself dangling from his fingertips.

'Got ya!' he said triumphantly.

'Let me go!' gasped Twink, twisting and kicking in his grasp.

Whipping out a jar from under the covers, Timmy popped Twink into it. She landed with a hard *thump* on the glass floor, and gaped in disbelief

as he screwed a lid on to the top.

Fluttering frantically, she beat on the smooth walls with both hands. 'Let me *go*,' she repeated. Her voice echoed faintly around her.

Timmy leered in at her, his face like a giant moon. 'No way!' he chortled. 'You're the ninth fairy in my collection. You look different from the others, though,' he added. Carrying her over to the night light, his eyes widened. 'Wow, you've got pink hair!'

'You horrid, horrid boy!' yelled Twink. She kicked the side of the jar as hard as she could. 'I thought you were *nice*!'

Timmy sniggered. 'Yeah, the note's ace, isn't it? Lures you lot in every time!' Taking a pair of scissors from his desk, he neatly snipped off the thread that still hung outside the jar. Twink struggled to stay upright as he carried her across the room.

'Where are you taking me?' she cried. 'Put me *down*!'

Timmy ignored her as he opened his wardrobe door. Climbing up on to a chair, he moved a shoebox on a shelf, shoved Twink's jar behind it, and then put the shoebox back into place.

'Stop!' shouted Twink, banging on the glass. 'What are you doing? You can't just *leave* me here.'

'Welcome to your new home,' sang Timmy. His voice was fading slightly, and she realised he was climbing down from the chair again. 'You'll love it, I promise. Just like all the others!'

The wardrobe door shut with a click . . . and the world went black around her. 'Wait!' screeched Twink, banging the glass with her fist. 'Wait!'

There was no response. Distantly, Twink heard Timmy get back into bed . . . and then a few minutes later came the sound of his snores. The horrible little boy had actually gone to sleep!

Defeated, Twink sank back on to her haunches. What on earth was she going to do now? She was trapped in here, alone in the dark.

All at once she straightened as hope tingled through her. What was it that Timmy had said? Something about 'the others' – and that she was the 'ninth fairy in his collection'! Could it be that she wasn't by herself after all?

'Is – is anybody there?' Twink whispered hesitantly.

'Yes,' answered a gloomy female voice.

Twink let out a relieved breath. Though she wouldn't have wished for anyone else to be trapped like she had been, she wasn't sorry to have some company in here! 'Are there really eight of you, like he said?' she asked.

'I suppose so,' said the voice. 'We've never bothered to count.'

Twink's eyes widened in surprise. How could they not know how many of them had been captured?

'Well – are you all tooth fairies?' she pressed.

'Yes,' came the reply. 'Aren't *you*?'

Twink sighed, and sat down on the hard glass floor. She didn't really want to talk about it very much – she felt silly enough already. 'No, I was just doing someone a favour,' she said. 'Anyway, I'm Twink. What's your name?'

'Midnight,' said the other fairy. 'It's nice that you've come,' she added politely. 'We were all getting very bored, just talking to each other. Do you know any good stories?'

Twink felt her jaw drop. Midnight spoke as if she planned on spending the rest of her life here! 'No, I don't,' she snapped. 'Midnight, what about *escaping*? What have you and the other fairies tried?'

'Escaping?' echoed the other fairy. 'Oh. Well, it's difficult, you see – the lids are always screwed on so tightly. But at least we have air holes. And Timmy brings us food every day. I suppose it's not *so* bad here . . .'

As Twink's eyes adjusted to the darkness, she could just make out another jar beside hers. She stared at it in disbelief. 'Not so bad?' she repeated. 'Are you mad? It's *awful*! What does he want with us, anyway?'

'I don't know. I think he just likes collecting things,' said Midnight.

'Haven't you ever *asked*?' said Twink in amazement.

There was a pause.

'Er . . . no,' said Midnight finally. 'Should we have?'

Twink gave up. What was wrong with these fairies, anyway? It was as if they were too dismal to even care. Maybe Shadow was a bit prickly, but at least she had some life to her!

'Well, I'm going to go to sleep now,' she said crossly.

'Goodnight,' said Midnight's voice. 'And do have a think about the stories, won't you, Twink? It would be lovely to hear some new ones.'

Twink didn't answer. She curled up on the hard glass floor, tucking her lavender wings tightly around her. Though she was trying not to feel too sorry for herself, it wasn't easy. If the other fairies were anything like Midnight, then having them here was almost worse than being alone!

It'll be all right, she told herself, staring out into the darkness. *When I don't come back, Bimi and Sooze will realise something's gone wrong, and they'll come looking for me.*

And poor Shadow! She'd probably feel dreadful when she found out what had happened. Twink yawned, beginning to feel sleepy despite her uncomfortable bed. Yes, someone would be coming after her soon . . . she was sure of it.

'The Brave One sensed there was a tooth that needed collecting – but then her heart sank as she realised whose tooth it was. What was she to do? She had to collect the tooth, but knew only too well the danger that awaited her!'

Twink cracked one eye open grumpily. Who was telling stories so late at night? For a confused moment she couldn't remember where she was, and then it all came flooding back. She groaned as she

sat up, straining to see in the dim light.

'Yes, be afraid!' continued the voice to its audience. 'For it was a name to inspire dread in all tooth fairies . . . *the Terrible Timmy.*'

Twink's eyes widened. Had the tooth fairies *known* that Timmy was going to try and capture them? But why on earth would they still come to his house, in that case?

'The Brave One had escaped the Terrible Timmy once before, but could she do it again? Stealthily, she crept into his room . . .'

Twink's thoughts spun. Could *Shadow* have been aware that Twink was flying into danger? But no, that couldn't be right! No one could be so horrid to someone who was only trying to help them – could they?

'The Brave One found the tooth, cut the thread that was tied around it . . . and then the Terrible Timmy pounced!'

Though the story had the feel of one that had been told many times before, a horrified gasp echoed about the wardrobe shelf. Twink craned her pointed ears, listening intently.

'The Brave One flew this way, she flew that way! Finally, she managed to escape with the tooth . . . but she vowed that she would never return to the Terrible Timmy's house again, if she could help it.'

The audience sighed with satisfaction. Suddenly a horrible suspicion came to Twink, and she leapt to her feet. 'Hang on!' she cried. 'Who's this *Brave One* you keep going on about?'

There was a startled pause. 'She is called Shadow,' said the storyteller finally, her voice hushed with respect. 'She's the only one of us to have escaped the Terrible Timmy.'

Oh! Twink's wings felt on fire with anger. 'Well, I don't think Shadow's brave at all!' she burst out. 'She *tricked* me into coming here, and never even told me to be careful! She –'

'Oh, Twink, tell us the story!' broke in Midnight's voice eagerly.

'Yes, please!' echoed several others.

Twink could have kicked her jar in frustration. Were stories all that these stupid fairies cared about?

Fine – she'd tell them one they'd never forget!

She plunged into her tale, beginning from when she'd first noticed the little branch at the top of Glitterwings. The tooth fairies hardly breathed as she described her journey up to it, the strange carvings on the shelf – and then meeting Shadow herself.

'So *that's* where the Brave One lives,' whispered an awestruck voice in the darkness. 'I've often wondered. And you say she *carves* things? How strange!'

Murmurs of agreement came from all directions. Twink gritted her teeth and carried on, describing Shadow's hurt wing – if it had really been hurt at all, that is – and how she and Sooze had offered to help.

'And Shadow never even told me to be careful,' she finished up indignantly, after describing her capture by Timmy. 'She knew perfectly well that I was flying into a trap, but she never warned me!'

There was silence on the darkened shelf. Finally the same fairy whose story had woken Twink up spoke. 'You must be mistaken,' she said.

'Yes, you must have got it wrong, somehow,' said Midnight's voice. 'Shadow is the Brave One! She wouldn't do such a thing.'

Twink opened her mouth to argue – and then slowly shut it again. Maybe the tooth fairies, trapped here in their jars, *needed* to believe in the Brave One for their own comfort.

'I suppose you're right,' she said after a pause. 'Maybe I – I didn't understand her, or something.'

'I'm sure that was it,' said Midnight, sounding relieved. 'But it was a good story anyway, Twink. Would you tell it again tomorrow?'

Twink sighed. 'No, I don't think so,' she said. 'My friends will be coming after me soon . . .'

She trailed off, suddenly wondering whether that was the case. After all, Sooze hadn't heard where she was going – Shadow had taken Twink to one side and whispered the directions. And what if Shadow refused to help them?

Twink straightened her wings. Well, whether her friends came to save her or not, she had no intention of staying here!

'When it's lighter, I'm going to try and escape,' she said firmly. 'Timmy will be at school during the day, won't he?' She remembered from her time with Lindsay that human children had to leave their homes every day to be taught.

'Yes, that's right,' said Midnight. 'I don't think you'll be able to escape, though, Twink. You might as well just accept it: you're here with us now.'

There were murmurs of agreement from the others. Twink clenched her jaw. 'Well, I think I'll at least try first, before I give up and live in a jar for the rest of my life!'

She could almost see Midnight's shrug. 'Suit yourself.'

To change the subject, Twink said, 'There's one thing I don't understand. Did you all know that Timmy was going to try and capture you?'

'Only some of us knew,' replied the storyteller. 'After the Brave One escaped for the first time, she told others what was happening. All we'd known until then was that sometimes tooth fairies went missing.'

'Oh,' said Twink in bewilderment. 'But why did you keep *coming* here, in that case?'

'It's because of the tooth fairy pact,' explained Midnight. 'We have a very old agreement with humans, you see. If there's a tooth that needs collecting, then we have to come and exchange a coin for it – no matter what.'

Twink frowned. 'But . . . why? I mean, why do you want their teeth?'

A startled gasp came from the darkness around her. 'Because we're tooth fairies!' cried the story-teller. 'That's what we do!'

'But do you *like* collecting teeth?' insisted Twink. 'At least Shadow carves things in hers – do you lot do anything like that?'

There was a confused silence.

'Um . . . we just collect them, that's all,' said a voice finally. 'It's what we've always done.'

'Yes. It is our fate,' said the storyteller.

For the second time that night, Twink gave up. She was starting to realise that tooth fairies were very different from ordinary fairies . . . and she wasn't sure that they could ever begin to understand each other!

Chapter
Five

'Sooze! Sooze, wake up!'

Someone was shaking her shoulder. 'Go away,' mumbled Sooze sleepily. She rolled over on to her side, pulling her bluebell-petal duvet around her.

'*Sooze!* We fell asleep! Twink's not back yet!' hissed Bimi.

Sooze awoke with a start. The last thing she remembered was lying in bed talking to Bimi, waiting for Twink to return – and now the sky outside their window was beginning to lighten. Twink had left *hours* ago!

She sprang out of bed, her heart thudding. 'Something must be wrong!' she whispered. Around them, the rest of Bluebell Branch lay sleeping. Sili's soft snores echoed across the ledge.

Bimi nodded anxiously. 'Sooze, I'm really scared. What if – what if she's hurt herself somehow, and can't get back?'

Sooze flung on her dressing gown. 'I'm going to go and see Shadow, and find out exactly where Twink went,' she said.

'I'm coming with you,' said Bimi, grabbing her own dressing gown.

Sooze glanced at her in surprise. 'Are you sure? The passageway's really tight in places –'

'Of course I'm sure!' Bimi looked close to tears. 'Twink's my best friend! If I had only gone along in the first place, this might not have happened.'

Sooze put her hands on her hips. 'What's *that* supposed to mean?'

Bimi blew out a breath. 'Nothing! It's just that – well, you do tend to egg each other on a bit, don't you?'

Sooze felt a pinch of guilt as she remembered that Twink hadn't even thought of going until she'd teased her into it. 'Well, never mind that now,' she muttered. 'Come on, let's go!'

Soon the two fairies had climbed up the narrow trunk and were pulling themselves on to the ledge. Sooze banged on the door with her fist. 'Shadow!' she yelled. 'Open up!'

There was no response. Sooze banged harder. 'SHADOW! We need to talk to you!'

'Let's just go in,' said Bimi, reaching for the door-knob. She turned it – and the door swung open.

The room was empty.

Flitting inside, Sooze stared around her in surprise. There was no sign of Shadow anywhere! Even the shelves where the carvings had stood were now bare. It was as if the tooth fairy had never been there at all.

'I don't like this one bit,' said Bimi. 'Where would she have gone, with a hurt wing?'

'If it really *was* hurt,' said Sooze grimly. She spotted something on the floor. 'Look, it's one of her carvings!' she exclaimed, holding the owl carving up. 'Bimi, I think she's packed up and left – she must have dropped this one on her way out.'

Bimi's pretty face paled. 'Then we have to go after her! She's the only one who knows where Twink is.'

'Yes, but how?' demanded Sooze fretfully. 'It's been hours already! She could be *anywhere* by now –'

The two of them froze as they heard the sound of wings approaching. Without a word, Sooze grabbed Bimi and pulled them both flat against the wall by the window.

Shadow landed on the sill, balancing herself with her silvery-grey wings as she swung the window open. Glancing furtively around her, she hopped to the floor. 'Now, where did it go . . . ?' she murmured.

'Looking for this?' asked Sooze, stepping forward. She held up the owl carving.

Shadow gasped as she whirled towards them. 'I – you –' she stammered.

'Where's Twink?' demanded Bimi coldly. 'She left hours ago!'

Shadow gulped. 'I – I'm sure she's all right,' she faltered, edging towards the window.

Sooze leapt in front of it, blocking the way. 'Yes, but where *is* she? Something's gone wrong, hasn't it?'

Shadow bit her lip. 'Um . . . maybe. It's sort of hard to tell . . .'

Sooze glared at her. What on earth was this silly fairy playing at? With a sudden inspiration, she held Shadow's carving out of the window. 'Tell us *now,* or I'll drop it!' she threatened.

'No!' burst out Shadow. She reached out an arm

65

as if unable to stop herself. 'You can't – that's my best one!'

'Watch me!' said Sooze. She dangled the owl loosely, swinging it back and forth. 'What do you think, Bimi? Will it break when it hits the ground?'

Bimi hated unpleasantness, but to Sooze's relief she played along. 'Maybe,' she said, folding her arms over her chest. 'Teeth are hard, but they *do* crack sometimes, don't they?'

Shadow pressed her hands against her mouth, her eyes wide with horror.

'Oh dear – wouldn't that be a shame, if it cracked to bits!' said Sooze. 'It's getting very heavy . . . I don't think I'll be able to hold on to it much longer . . .'

'Stop!' shrieked Shadow. 'All right, I'll tell you, I'll tell you!'

Sooze brought the owl carving back inside. 'Go on, then,' she said. 'Where's Twink? And tell us the truth, mind, or out of the window it goes!'

Shadow gulped, her eyes on her precious carving. 'She – she may have got into a bit of trouble. You

see . . . the tooth she went to collect belonged to the Terrible Timmy.'

Sooze stared. 'The *who*?'

The tooth fairy wrung her hands as she explained about the human boy and his collection of fairies. 'You mean Twink's been captured?' gasped Bimi.

'You horrible thing!' burst out Sooze. 'You never even warned her – I ought to throw your stupid carving right out of the window!'

'Yes, and then you sneaked off so that you wouldn't have to face us,' said Bimi, looking angrier than Sooze had ever seen her. 'You didn't even *have* a hurt wing, did you?'

'No,' Shadow mumbled. 'I – I was scared, that's all. I've escaped the Terrible Timmy twice, but what if I couldn't do it again? He almost got me last time! Just the thought of being trapped in a jar makes me go into a cold sweat.'

'Well, how do you think it makes Twink feel?' demanded Sooze fiercely. 'Now, where's this house?'

Shadow looked taken aback. 'You mean – you're going after her? But it's really dangerous there. You could both be trapped yourselves!'

'Well, we'll have to take that chance,' said Bimi shortly. 'Twink's our friend.'

Sooze nodded. 'Come on, Shadow. You're going to show us exactly where this house is.'

The tooth fairy went snowy pale. '*Now?*' she squeaked. 'But it's practically daylight!'

'So?' said Bimi, flitting to the window. 'It's still really early; no one will be up for ages yet. Come on, let's go!'

Shadow tugged anxiously at her black and grey dress. 'But I'm a night fairy!' she cried. 'I can't fly in the daylight for more than a few minutes without getting dizzy. Can't I just *tell* you where the house is?'

'No,' said Sooze firmly. She tucked the carving into the belt of her dressing gown. 'I don't trust you one little bit, Shadow. Dizzy or not, you're coming with us – now!'

Climbing through the window one after the other, the three fairies took off from the branch. Following

Shadow's directions they flew across the nearby meadow, and then turned and headed over a small cluster of trees. Soon a line of human houses became visible on the horizon.

'It's one of those,' said Shadow faintly, pointing towards them. Her wing strokes had become weaker and weaker as they flew, and now she kept pressing her hand against her forehead as though it pained her.

'Sooze, she doesn't look very well,' whispered Bimi, swooping close. 'Maybe we should let her go back.'

'We can't!' hissed Sooze. 'What if it's a trick?'

Suddenly Shadow gave a cry. Her silvery-grey wings faltered . . . and then stopped fluttering altogether. She plummeted towards the earth, tumbling through the air like a stone.

Sooze and Bimi dived after the tooth fairy, and just managed to grab her before she hit the ground. 'Shadow!' cried Bimi, laying her down on the grass and shaking her gently. 'Are you OK?'

'Too bright,' mumbled Shadow, closing her eyes.

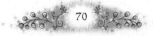

'I can't . . .' She trailed off, her head lolling limply to one side.

Bimi slapped Shadow's wrists lightly. 'Oh, Sooze, she's passed out!' she wailed. 'What are we going to do now?'

Sooze stared worriedly at the houses, wondering which one Twink was in, and whether she was all right. She took a deep breath. 'I never thought I'd say this, but – but I think we'd better fly back and tell one of the teachers,' she said.

Bimi nodded, scrambling to her feet. 'You're right. We were total moss brains not to go to them the

moment Twink didn't return!' She grabbed hold of Shadow's arms. 'Come on, Sooze, take her legs. We'd better get her back to Glitterwings as quickly as we can.'

Chapter Six

Twink sighed as she glared up at the lid of her jar. Though she hadn't been trying long, her arm and wing muscles already ached from attempting to unscrew it. Somehow she *would* manage to do it, she promised herself, slumping back on to the floor. She just had to rest a bit first.

It was morning now, and Twink could see the inside of the wardrobe a little more clearly. Eight other jars stood in the shadows around her, each holding a fairy that looked similar to Shadow – pale skin, dark hair and gloomy-looking clothes.

Midnight turned out to have soft brown eyes and shoulder-length black hair. 'I've told you, you can't escape,' she called, leaning against the wall of her jar. 'Are you convinced now?'

Twink gave her a sour look. 'I've only tried a few times – I'm not about to give up yet!'

'Oh.' Midnight shrugged. 'It's just that you look really tired.'

Twink didn't reply. Fluttering to the top of the jar again, she propped her hands against the lid and pushed with all her might. Her wings beat madly as she shoved and strained.

All at once she slipped, and crashed against the smooth glass wall. 'Ouch!' she muttered crossly. There had to be a better way to do this!

There was a click, and the wardrobe door swung open. Twink gasped, shielding her eyes in the sudden light. The tooth fairies sat up, looking more alert than Twink had seen them yet.

'Breakfast time,' said Midnight, rubbing her wings together in anticipation.

There was a scraping noise like a chair being

pulled up to the wardrobe, and then the shoebox was taken away. Timmy's face appeared, grinning in at them. 'Good morning, fairies!' he sang.

One by one, he began picking up the jars, unscrewing the lids and dropping in a bit of bread. Each fairy got a thimbleful of water, too, lowered down by a thread until they'd drunk their fill. Twink watched in amazement. Why on earth weren't any of them trying to *escape*?

'Now it's *your* turn, Pinky,' said Timmy.

Twink bristled at the awful name, but she had more important things to think about. She watched carefully as he picked up her jar, waiting for her chance. The moment he raised the lid, she flew upwards in a rush.

'Hey!' Startled, Timmy quickly slammed the lid shut again. Twink let out a squawk as she banged her head on it.

The Terrible Timmy peered in at her, his eye almost half as large as she was. 'That wasn't very nice,' he said. 'I'm only trying to give you your breakfast!'

Twink scowled at him. Though she could see that he was very young, she hardly thought *that* was an excuse for not understanding that she'd rather be out of the jar, getting her own breakfast!

Before she could respond, he'd opened the lid a tiny crack and shoved the bit of bread through. She spluttered in rage as it dropped on her head, but the Terrible Timmy had already screwed the lid tightly shut again.

'I'd better save your water until you're not so naughty, Pinky,' he decided, placing Twink's jar back on the shelf. 'Bye, fairies – see you after school!' And

a moment later the wardrobe had been cast into gloom again, with the shoebox back in place and the door firmly shut.

'What's *wrong* with you lot?' shouted Twink, kicking the piece of bread at her feet. They stopped eating and looked at her in surprise.

'What do you mean?' asked Midnight. She wiped a crumb from her mouth. 'If we tried to escape, then we wouldn't get fed – just like *you* didn't get any water. It's not worth it.'

'Of course it's worth it!' cried Twink. 'Wouldn't you *like* to escape? Just imagine flying again! Stretching your wings and – and feeling the breeze blowing through your hair –'

She stopped, swallowing hard. Oh, what would she do if she *didn't* manage to get out of this jar? And why hadn't her friends come after her by now?

One by one, the tooth fairies had stopped eating. 'Of course we'd like those things,' said Midnight softly, staring down at her bread. Her large eyes looked deeply sad. 'It's just not possible, so – so I suppose we've given up trying.'

'Yes, and we don't need *you* reminding us of it all,' said the storyteller, who Twink had found out was called Moonbeam. She was a sharp-faced fairy with grey wings, which she was fluttering crossly. 'You don't know what it's like for us – most of us have been here for ages!'

'But that's just my point,' protested Twink. 'Maybe you don't have to be! There *must* be a way to –'

She broke off as Moonbeam turned her back on her. 'Who wants to hear the story of the tooth fairy who forgot her coin?' she asked the others.

The fairies sighed in relief, clearly glad to put Twink and escaping out of their minds. They settled down on their floors, nibbling their bits of bread.

'Once upon a time there was a very forgetful fairy,' started Moonbeam. 'She forgot everything! She forgot to comb her hair in the morning, and she forgot to put on her shoes, and –'

Twink bit her lip as the story continued. None of the tooth fairies were looking at her – not even Midnight.

I didn't mean to upset them, she thought in

bewilderment. She couldn't understand it. It was as if the tooth fairies were so frightened they wouldn't be able to escape that they'd rather not try at all.

Well, I can't give up that easily, Twink told herself firmly. *I* am *going to get out of here – and that's all there is to it!*

Looking down at her bread, she sighed and sat down to eat. Though dry bread without any water wasn't very nice, she knew that she needed to keep her strength up. She had a long, hard day ahead of her.

'Oomph!' grunted Twink.

Her jar rocked from side to side as she flung herself about inside it. She paused, breathing hard. Had the shoebox moved slightly? She couldn't be certain, but she thought maybe it had.

After trying for hours, Twink had finally decided the tooth fairies were right – it wasn't possible to unscrew the lid from the inside. That left only one thing that she could think of: she would break the jar itself, by making it fall on to the floor. But first, she had to get rid of the shoebox blocking her way.

Setting her jaw, Twink threw herself about again, rocking the jar wildly. It thumped against the shoebox. This time she definitely felt the box edge forward, and she grinned. Ha! Almost there!

The tooth fairies had finished their story ages ago, and now just sat staring at her, clearly convinced that she was mad. Twink paid them no attention as she bumped her jar from side to side. The shoebox slid forward jerkily.

'Er, Twink . . . what are you doing?' asked Midnight.

'Trying to knock the shoebox off the shelf,' said Twink shortly, stopping to rest for a moment.

The tooth fairies gasped in horror. 'But the Terrible Timmy will notice!' squeaked Midnight. 'He won't be very pleased, Twink.'

'Well, with any luck, I won't be here to talk to him about it,' muttered Twink.

She started rocking again, even harder than before. Her jar practically skipped forward, nudging the shoebox further and further off the shelf. Finally the box teetered at the edge, almost ready to drop.

Gritting her teeth, Twink banged against the side of her jar. The box slid over the edge, vanishing from view. *CRASH!* The sound echoed across the shelf as it hit the wardrobe floor.

'Hurrah!' shouted Twink, punching the air. Now it would be the easiest thing in the world to rock *herself* over the shelf's edge. She just hoped that she could avoid being hurt when the jar shattered on the wardrobe floor.

I'll have to fly away the moment it hits the ground, Twink told herself. She began rocking again, bumping her shoulder against the glass. The jar scooted towards the shelf edge.

'Twink . . . are you *sure* that's a good idea?' called Midnight.

'It's the only . . . idea . . . I have,' grunted Twink. Bump! Bump! Her jar crept forward.

Midnight was pressed against the side of her jar, her face screwed up with worry. 'Yes, but what happens when –'

Whoosh! Suddenly Twink was hurtling through

the air. There was a tremendous *THUMP* as the jar landed, slamming her against its smooth wall – and then everything went still.

Twink got up shakily, looking around her. Why hadn't the jar broken?

Then she saw what had happened, and groaned in dismay. The shoebox had burst open when it hit the wardrobe floor – and now her jar had plopped right into one of the shoes, rising up out of it like a sail from a boat.

'*No!*' cried Twink, smacking her forehead with her fist. How unlucky could she get?

'Twink?' came Midnight's voice from above. 'Are you OK?'

'I'm fine,' Twink called back crossly.

There was a pause. 'I didn't hear the jar break,' said Midnight.

'That's because it didn't – I'm still trapped,' Twink answered. She slumped down on to the floor, propping her chin in her hands.

Thankfully, Midnight didn't say 'I told you so'. 'Well . . . what are you going to do now?' she asked.

Twink traced a pattern on the glass floor. Though she hadn't given up, she had no idea what to try next. Plus she was terribly thirsty, which didn't help at all.

'I don't know,' she admitted. 'I – I suppose I'll just listen to one of Moonbeam's stories . . . if she'll tell one.'

The day passed slowly, even with Moonbeam's tales. No wonder the tooth fairies enjoyed stories so much, realised Twink as she stifled a yawn. It was so *boring* in here! At least listening to a story took your mind off things for a while.

Though it was hard to be certain from inside the wardrobe, she sensed that it was early evening – and still there was no sign of Timmy. 'Sometimes he has activity clubs after school,' Midnight told her. 'But he always comes back sooner or later.'

'Great,' muttered Twink, wondering what Timmy would say when he saw that she'd tried to escape. If she were lucky, maybe he'd decide that she was too much trouble, and unscrew the lid and set her free!

I don't think that's very likely, though, thought Twink glumly. Suddenly her eyes narrowed. Maybe Timmy wouldn't set her free on purpose – but could she somehow *trick* him into opening the lid?

For a moment Twink's wings shivered with excitement . . . and then she let out a breath. That was all right for her, but what about the other fairies? She was starting to realise that she couldn't just leave them here – they were so dispirited that they'd never escape on their own.

Moonbeam started another story. Twink only half listened as she turned the problem over in her mind. There *must* be a way that she could rescue not only herself, but the others, too!

'Vera was the most nervous tooth fairy in the world,' Moonbeam was saying from above. 'Why, she was even frightened of the teeth she was supposed to collect!'

Twink smiled despite herself, reminded of Mr Woodleaf. He was practically scared of his own shadow unless he was with his beloved animals. Then he was braver than anyone. Like in their last lesson, when he'd brought the badger out –

Suddenly Twink gasped as she remembered the glamour that Mariella had cast. *Of course!* Why hadn't she thought of it sooner? If she could just get Timmy to let her out of the jar, then perhaps she could use fairy magic to rescue the others.

I'll have to plan it out really carefully, thought Twink. What sort of glamour should she cast? Whatever illusion she chose, it would have to be perfect – and very distracting!

Maybe the others will have some ideas, she thought. But before she could ask them, someone came into the bedroom.

Abruptly, Moonbeam stopped telling her story. Silence fell over the wardrobe as every fairy in it craned to hear. 'Thanks, Mum,' called Timmy's voice. It sounded like he was eating something. 'These are great.'

Twink winced in the sudden light as the wardrobe door swung open. Timmy's feet and legs appeared in front of her. She tilted her head back, trying to see his face.

'Hello, fairies! Sorry I'm so late getting home, but – *hey*!' broke off Timmy. 'What's happened? Where's the shoebox?'

'It wasn't us!' Twink heard Moonbeam pipe up. 'It was –'

'Sshhh!' said Midnight fiercely.

The Terrible Timmy had already worked it out for himself. Squatting down, he peered in at Twink in her jar. She gulped hard.

'Hello, Pinky,' he said. 'Have you been having fun?'

Chapter Seven

Twink held back a squawk as Timmy picked up her jar and carried her over to his desk. Anger sizzled through her as she saw that he was eating some sort of chocolate biscuit. He could at least offer her a bite – she'd only had a bit of bread all day!

But he popped the last morsel into his mouth without seeming to give it a thought. 'You're different from the other fairies,' he announced, brushing chocolate crumbs from his chin. 'Are you the same sort as them?'

Twink shrugged, her thoughts racing. Somehow,

she had to get him to unscrew the lid and let her out – but how? She held back a shriek as he picked up her jar again, turning it this way and that.

'The others look really drab compared with you,' said Timmy. He looked wistful. 'I wish I had more fairies like *you* in my collection.'

An idea started to form in Twink's mind. She swallowed hard, wondering if it could possibly work. But she had no other choice than to try.

She raised an eyebrow as if she were surprised. 'More fairies like me?' she echoed. 'But what for? *I'm* nothing special. There are loads of other fairies who are much more interesting.'

Timmy stared at her. 'Really?'

'Of course,' said Twink. 'I'm just a boring old nature fairy – you can get one of us anywhere. And as for those tooth fairies up in your wardrobe . . .' She *tsk*ed, shaking her head. 'Really, Timmy! I don't know what you're bothering with *that* lot for.'

'What do you mean?' demanded Timmy, looking hurt. 'I've got a *great* fairy collection.'

'Well . . .' Twink pulled a face.

'I have!' insisted Timmy. He shook her jar slightly, scowling.

'Oh, it's all right, I suppose,' yawned Twink. 'But if you want a really good collection, you should get some sparkle fairies. They're the rarest fairies in the world. *Nobody* else has a sparkle fairy collection!'

An almost hungry look crossed Timmy's face. He lifted up her jar, peering in at her. 'What are sparkle fairies?'

Twink had no idea, since no such thing existed! She thought fast. 'They come in all different colours,' she said. 'And they sparkle when they fly. In fact, they – they glow in the dark, like little stars!'

Timmy's jaw dropped. '*Glow in the dark?* Wow! How can I get some?'

'It wouldn't be easy,' said Twink thoughtfully. 'They're very shy. But if you like, I could summon some for you. Only you'd have to let me out of the jar first.' She held her breath, hardly daring to move while Timmy thought it over.

'You couldn't summon them from inside the jar?' he said finally.

Twink shook her head so hard that her pink hair tumbled about her face. 'No, I need room to move about,' she told him firmly.

'All right,' decided Timmy. 'Only I'd better shut the window first.' He put her jar down, and Twink watched in dismay as he went across and swung the bedroom window closed. *Never mind*, she told herself. If her plan succeeded, then they'd work out how to open the window once they got to it!

There was a *whoosh* of air as the Terrible Timmy unscrewed Twink's lid. 'Come on, then,' he said eagerly, tipping her out on to the desk.

Twink fluttered from the jar, breathing deeply. She had never dreamed that fresh air could taste so good!

'All right, I just need to – to prepare myself,' she said.

Her thoughts were racing. Though Mariella was very good at glamours and could cast them practically from thin air, she herself needed to have some sort of object in place, which she could then disguise as something else. What, though? She looked around the room, trying desperately to find something.

'What are you waiting for?' demanded Timmy.

He moved the lamp on his desk, adjusting it so that its beam shone right on her. All at once Twink could see hundreds of tiny dust motes floating past. She grinned. Suddenly she knew exactly what she was going to do!

'All right, I'm ready,' she said.

Closing her eyes, Twink began to move her hands in the complicated patterns of the spell, carefully imagining what the sparkle fairies would look like. She made them just her size, and in all different colours, glimmering like tiny rainbows.

'WHOA!' shouted Timmy. He sprang up from his chair with a clatter.

Twink opened her eyes and saw him leaping about the room, trying fruitlessly to grab dust motes. Though Twink couldn't be fooled by her own spell, she knew that to Timmy, the bedroom was now filled with dancing, swirling sparkle fairies – which would be *very* difficult to catch!

She jetted to the wardrobe. Thankfully, its door still stood open. Hurrying to Midnight's jar, she landed on the rim and started pushing at the lid. But it was too smooth for her hands to get a grip on.

'Twink, what are you doing?' hissed Midnight. 'Just fly away! If Timmy catches you –'

Twink ignored her. She needed something to grasp it with, somehow! Remembering an object she'd seen on the desk, she swooped back to grab it, and a moment later was back at Midnight's jar again, pulling a rubber band around the lid.

'Stay still!' bellowed Timmy, snatching at the air. 'I almost had you that time!'

The rubber band gave Twink a firm grip that hadn't been possible on the slippery metal. This time when she pushed at the lid, she thought it moved a tiny bit. Beating her wings as hard as she could, she shoved and strained. The lid seemed to hesitate – and then suddenly came loose in a rush.

Hurrah! Twink pushed it off the jar. Midnight stood inside, blinking up at her. 'You did it,' she gasped. 'Oh, Twink, you're brilliant!'

'Hurry,' whispered Twink. 'You have to help me with the others!'

She returned to the desk for another rubber band, dodging past Timmy's flailing hands. He hardly seemed to notice her – he was too busy grabbing at the 'sparkle fairies'!

When she returned to the wardrobe, Midnight had already set another of the fairies free. Working together, they flitted from jar to jar, unscrewing the lids. The tooth fairies flew out of their prisons in a daze.

When Twink reached Moonbeam's jar, the prickly fairy bit her lip in fright. 'Oh, Twink – what will he do if he sees us –'

Twink pushed off her lid. 'Let's not stay and find out!' she said. 'The spell will last for a few minutes yet – come on!'

Peering out from the wardrobe, Twink waited until the Terrible Timmy had his back to them, and then she motioned for the others to follow. They flew towards the window in a straggling line.

To Twink's alarm, some of the tooth fairies weren't flying very well – it was obvious that they hadn't stretched their wings properly in ages. She had to get them out of here before Timmy spotted them!

Reaching the window, Twink saw with relief that it was worked by a simple latch. 'Midnight, help me!' she cried. Fluttering madly, the two of them pulled down on the latch until it opened with a *click,* and then flew forward, pushing with all their might. The window swung open.

'Hurry, hurry!' cried Twink.

The tooth fairies flew past her out of the open

window. 'Oh! It's so lovely!' breathed one of them.

Timmy's face was red with frustration. 'Stay STILL!' he shouted at the air, stamping his foot on the carpet. 'This isn't fair! I only want a few of you!'

Twink darted out of the window last of all. Suddenly she was hovering above the long garden that she remembered. It was twilight, with the first few stars just beginning to appear in the darkening sky.

'NO!' came an agonised shout. Twink turned and looked, her heart thudding. In the bedroom behind her, she could see Timmy gaping around him in dismay. 'They've gone!' he cried.

The spell had ended! Twink whirled about. 'Fly!' she shouted. 'Fly as fast as you can!'

'Oh, Twink – I can't, my wing –' gasped Moonbeam. She was grimacing with pain, her left wing faltering as she tried to flutter.

Twink darted to her side, putting an arm around her. 'Come on, I'll fly with you. The rest of you – go, go!'

97

'MY FAIRIES HAVE ESCAPED!' howled Timmy from the bedroom.

Glancing back, Twink saw him hanging out of the window, glaring right at her. 'You tricked me!' he bellowed, shaking his fist. He vanished abruptly, and Twink heard his bedroom door bang shut.

Moonbeam let out a little moan of terror, clenching her eyes shut. 'Oh, I knew this would happen – I just knew it –'

Twink gave her a shake. 'Stop that! Come on and *fly*, or neither of us has a chance!'

Midnight appeared, putting her arm around Moonbeam's other side. 'Come on, I'll help,' she said. 'Fly, Moonbeam! We can't let Timmy capture us again, after all the time we spent in that wardrobe!'

Feebly, Moonbeam began to fly, with Twink and Midnight helping her along. Most of the other fairies were already far ahead of them, barely visible now in the twilight.

'Mum! I'm just going out in the garden for a bit!' yelled Timmy's voice. He shot out of the back door,

shining a torch and looking wildly about him. Twink's blood ran cold as she saw that he had a jam jar in his hand.

'Keep high, so that he can't reach us!' she hissed.

But Moonbeam's wing strokes were becoming weaker and weaker – and though she wasn't very large, it was difficult to fly while supporting her. To Twink's dismay, they were losing height by the second.

An explosion of light burst around them, and Twink winced. Timmy had found them with his torch!

'It's *you* I want,' said Timmy, scowling at Twink. 'You're the one who can do magic and summon the sparkle fairies!'

He jumped up in the air, trying to scoop Twink into the jam jar. She shrieked and jerked backwards, fluttering as hard as she could to hold on to Moonbeam.

'Twink, go on!' shouted Midnight. 'It's not us he wants – just go, get away!'

'Aaarrgghh!' yelled Twink as the jar whistled towards her once more. Then she was hurtling through the air in a confused rush, flattened against its glass floor. She had been captured again!

'Ha! Thought you'd escaped, didn't you?' crowed Timmy.

Chapter Eight

Twink stared in dismay as Timmy screwed the lid on tightly. *No!* This couldn't be happening!

She could just make out the tooth fairies. Drawn by the commotion, they had flown back again, and were now watching the scene with horror on their pale faces.

Timmy turned away again, heading back towards the house with Twink. 'We're going to have *lots* of fun, Pinky,' he said. 'Now that I know you can do magic, I can get you to do all sorts!'

'No!' shouted a voice behind them. Suddenly

Twink could see a fairy fluttering in front of Timmy, beating her wings in his face. It was Midnight!

'Let her go!' she screamed, kicking his nose with her pixie boot. 'You've no right! Come on, you lot – are you going to let him take her after she helped us to escape?'

Twink saw the tooth fairies glance fearfully at each other. 'She's right!' cried Moonbeam, clutching her sore wing. 'Help her, everyone, help her!'

The fairies hesitated – and then seemed to decide all at once. As one, they started flying at Timmy, darting in his face as Midnight had done. He took a step back, looking alarmed. 'Hey! Stop that!'

'Let her go!' ordered Midnight. She yanked hard at a lock of his blond hair.

'Ow! Get off!' Swatting at his head, Timmy started to run. Twink shrieked, jolted about in her jar like a twig in a stream.

'Stop!' called a different voice. 'Grab his trouser legs, everyone – hurry!'

There was a confused blur as several new fairies darted on to the scene, zooming past Twink as they

joined the tooth fairies. 'Yes, there!' shouted the voice. 'One, two, three – PULL!'

'OOF!' shouted Timmy.

The world lurched crazily as he fell. The jar catapulted out of his hand, and Twink watched helplessly as she hurtled towards the ground. Suddenly, with a mad beating of wings, three fairies appeared beneath her, stopping the jar's fall.

'Bimi! Sooze! *Miss Shimmery!*' gasped Twink as they lowered her to the earth. A moment later they had unscrewed her lid, and Twink flew shakily out.

'Are you all right, my dear?' asked Miss Shimmery gently.

Twink nodded. All at once her throat felt choked with tears, and she couldn't speak.

'Good,' said Miss Shimmery, patting her shoulder. 'In that case I'd better go and see if the tooth fairies need any help. Take care of her, you two.'

She flitted off, and Bimi flung herself at Twink, hugging her hard. 'Oh, we were so worried!' she burst out. 'Shadow said that Timmy didn't hurt the fairies he caught, but –'

'*Shadow?*' repeated Twink in surprise. 'Is *she* here?'

Sooze nodded. 'It was her idea to trip up that horrible boy. You should have seen her – she flew at him like a whole army of wasps!' Suddenly she embraced Twink tightly. 'I'm really glad you're OK, Opposite. And next time, don't listen to me when I try to talk you into something!'

'But what happened?' asked Twink in wonder.

Quickly, Bimi and Sooze filled her in on all that had taken place while she had been captured. 'Miss Shimmery was brilliant,' said Sooze. 'She didn't scold us once; she just took care of Shadow.'

Bimi nodded. 'And then as soon as it was evening again and Shadow was well, she let Sooze and me come along to help rescue you.'

'Well, she couldn't have stopped us, really,' said Sooze with a grin.

'Leave me alone!' cried a voice.

Turning, Twink could see Timmy lying on the ground a short distance away, struggling to get up. The tooth fairies kept buzzing about his face, flapping and fluttering. 'Stop it!' he cried tearfully. 'Just go away!'

Shadow put her hands on her hips. 'No, we won't,' she said firmly. 'Not unless you promise to leave us alone from now on!'

Timmy nodded, his mouth trembling with fright.

Miss Shimmery was hovering to one side, her expression grave. 'I'm afraid that you've brought this on yourself, young human,' she told him. 'It's an evil thing to keep fairies captive, you know.'

Shadow swooped closer, looking fierce. 'Yes, and just to make sure you keep your promise, whenever you have a tooth that needs collecting from now on, at least a dozen of us will come for it – and if you ever try to catch any of us again, you'll be sorry! Is that clear?'

Timmy gulped. 'Y-yes,' he whispered. Though Twink knew that the awful little boy deserved this, she couldn't help feeling a bit sorry for him. He looked completely terrified!

'Good,' snapped Shadow. 'All right, everyone – let him get up.'

The tooth fairies retreated. Timmy didn't wait to be told again – he scrambled to his feet and ran into the house as fast as he could, banging the door shut behind him.

Sooze burst out laughing. 'Somehow I don't think he'll be collecting fairies any more!' she said. 'Maybe he should try something safer, like flowers.'

'Oh, I can't believe I did that!' Shadow gasped, pressing her hands to her cheeks. 'I – I actually stood up to him!'

The other tooth fairies looked at her in surprise. 'What do you mean?' asked Moonbeam. 'Of course you stood up to him. You're the Brave –'

'*Don't call me that!*' burst out Shadow. She looked close to tears. The other tooth fairies stared at her, their faces stricken.

Shadow gave a humourless laugh. 'The Brave One – ha, that's a joke! I'm anything *but* brave. In fact, I – I tricked Twink into coming here to collect the tooth for me, just because I was too scared to come myself.'

'You did?' echoed Moonbeam. 'But we thought . . .' She trailed off. Twink felt a pang of pity, remembering how much it had meant to the tooth fairies to hear about 'The Brave One' in their captivity.

'It's true,' said Shadow heavily. 'And even before this happened I was never brave. That's why I went to live in that empty branch at Glitterwings. Because I *hate* being called the Brave One, when I'm really such a coward!'

'But, Shadow, you have much more courage than you realise,' pointed out Miss Shimmery. 'You brought us straight here, and, despite your fear, you led the attack against the Terrible Timmy. Bravery doesn't mean not being frightened – it's the actions you take, whether you're frightened or not.'

Shadow hesitated. 'I suppose so, but . . . well, my actions towards Twink were still pretty cowardly, weren't they?' She turned to face Twink, her cheeks pink with shame. 'I'm sorry,' she said. 'No matter how scared I was, it was awful of me to ask you to come here without telling you about the danger. I wouldn't blame you if you hated me for it.'

Twink managed a smile. 'No, I don't hate you,' she said. 'And at least you came back and helped fight off Timmy. But, Shadow . . . what will you do now?'

'I don't know,' said Shadow, looking at the ground. 'I've been pretty lonely at Glitterwings. What I'd like most is to go back with the other tooth fairies . . . if they don't mind that I'm not really all that brave.'

There was a startled silence.

'I – I suppose being the Brave One would be a lot for *any* of us to live up to,' said Moonbeam finally. 'I'm sorry if we made you feel uncomfortable,

Shadow. We'd like very much to have you back.'

'Yes, we've really missed you!' burst out Midnight. 'And I'd love to hear more about your carvings. Whatever gave you the idea to do such a thing?'

Shadow ducked her head shyly. 'I don't know,' she said. 'I started carving things because I was lonely, but . . . then it just seemed to me as though the teeth *should* have things carved in them.' She made a face. 'I know that sounds mad.'

'Not at all,' said Miss Shimmery in her low voice. 'I did some reading about tooth fairies today, and that's how the pact between humans and tooth fairies first began. The tooth fairies have always been artists – and their favourite things to make art with have always been teeth.'

The tooth fairies looked stunned. '*Really?*' said Moonbeam. 'But – but if that's true, then it's been forgotten for years and years! None of *us* have ever made art. We just collect teeth because . . . well, because we always have.'

Miss Shimmery lifted her rainbow wings. 'It's a shame that your love of art has been lost,' she said.

'But it seems to me that you should be able to find it again . . . with Shadow's help.'

The tooth fairies stared at each other, and then slowly turned and looked at Shadow. 'Carving things,' mused Moonbeam. 'I've never thought of it before, but it sounds really interesting.'

'Yes, Shadow, would you teach us how?' asked Midnight. The other tooth fairies crowded about, echoing agreement.

Shadow's face was flushed with pleasure. 'Of course, if you want me to!' she said.

'Yes, please,' said Moonbeam firmly. 'I can see now that we tooth fairies have become very gloomy and set in our ways over the years. Something new to think about is exactly what we need.' Then she grinned. 'And just imagine, now we'll have a *reason* to collect teeth. It'll make it so much more fun!'

The tooth fairies talked excitedly to each other, their eyes shining. Looking at them, Twink could scarcely believe that these were the same fairies who, just a few hours ago, had been too downhearted to even *think* about escaping!

Midnight gave Twink a warm smile. 'And I think we could learn something from Twink, too, about being more positive,' she pointed out. 'Why, if it wasn't for her, we'd still be stuck in that wardrobe.'

'Yes, three cheers for Twink!' said Moonbeam.

Twink's face grew hot as the tooth fairies *hip-hip-hooray*ed her, fluttering their silvery wings. 'That's OK,' she said awkwardly. 'I was happy to help.'

And all at once it was true. Though it had been horrible being a captive, she was delighted that the tooth fairies were free now, and so much happier. Perhaps it was lucky that Shadow had tricked her, after all.

The two groups of fairies said goodbye to each other. 'Thanks for everything, Twink,' said Midnight, hugging her tightly.

Twink nodded, too emotional to speak. The tooth fairies were like old friends now, and suddenly she realised that she was going to miss them very much.

Then she remembered something, and pulled the bag from her shoulder. 'Here,' she said, wiping her eyes as she handed it to Shadow. 'This is yours.'

Shadow grinned. Opening the bag, she took out Timmy's tooth and turned it this way and that. 'Thanks – I'll have to carve something extra-special in this one! Goodbye, Twink.' She clasped Twink's hand. 'I hope I'll see you again sometime.'

She and the other tooth fairies flew away then, waving over their shoulders. Twink stood waving back until she couldn't see them any longer. Finally she dropped her arm with a sigh.

Sooze was hovering next to her, looking thoughtful. 'Where do tooth fairies live, anyway?' she asked.

Miss Shimmery adjusted her sparkle specs. 'I must confess to not knowing a great deal about tooth fairies before today, when I did some research,' she said. 'They're quite a strange branch of the fairy family, but very fascinating! To answer your question, Sooze, they normally live in garden sheds.'

'Garden sheds?' repeated Bimi in surprise.

The HeadFairy nodded. 'Yes – they like to be near humans so that they don't have far to go to collect their teeth. Shall we return to school now, girls? It's very late.'

The fairies took off into the warm summer night, skimming over the trees at the bottom of the garden. The stars stretched above them in a sea of lights.

'Bimi, you and Sooze fly on ahead a bit,' said Miss Shimmery. 'I want to have a private word with Twink.'

Twink gulped as her friends flew slowly away, looking worriedly over their shoulders. In all the excitement, she'd forgotten that she was likely to be in a great deal of trouble for sneaking out!

Still, she thought glumly, she probably deserved it. She was a fourth-year student now, and really ought to have known better. 'I'm sorry, Miss Shimmery,' she said. 'It was a daft thing to do. I – I know that I'll deserve any punishment you give me.'

Miss Shimmery's snowy white eyebrows rose. 'Is it daft to want to help someone, then?' she asked mildly. 'Shadow told me what she'd said to you.'

Twink squirmed. 'No, but . . . well, helping Shadow wasn't the only reason I went,' she admitted. 'I wanted a bit of excitement, too.'

Miss Shimmery smiled. 'Ah, now we're getting somewhere! Thank you for being so honest, Twink. Yes, it *is* exciting to leave school at night – but as you've seen, it can also be very dangerous.'

That was certainly true, thought Twink. She couldn't hold back a shudder as she remembered the Terrible Timmy's leering face.

'Now, I do understand what it's like to be a young fairy at school,' continued Miss Shimmery, 'and so I try to turn a blind eye to things like midnight jaunts to the Dingly Dell – within reason, of course! However, this was something very different, as I think you'll agree. The outcome might have been disastrous.'

Twink's wings felt heavy with guilt. 'I know,' she whispered. 'I – I'm sorry.'

Miss Shimmery's sparkle specs caught the moonlight as she gazed at her. 'If you were me, Twink, what sort of punishment would you give to a student who did what you did?' she asked.

Startled, Twink tried to think. 'Well – I'd want it to be serious enough so that she wouldn't do it again,' she said slowly. 'But I'd want her to really have to think about what she'd done as well, so that she'd see why it was wrong.'

Miss Shimmery nodded approvingly. 'Yes, that's what I think, too. Would you agree, Twink, that restricting your free time for a month, plus asking you to write a report on the dangers of sneaking out at night, might accomplish both of those things?'

The punishment was far milder than she'd been expecting. Twink nodded in relief. 'Yes, Miss Shimmery.'

The HeadFairy smiled. 'That's what we'll do, then. And, Twink . . . I was talking to some of the tooth fairies before, and I'm very impressed at how you helped them to escape. Well done, my dear – you acted with both courage and resourcefulness.'

Twink's pointed ears grew warm at the praise. 'Thank you,' she said. Embarrassed, she quickly changed the subject. 'Miss Shimmery, there's one thing I still don't understand. What was that little branch at the top of the tree first used for?'

The HeadFairy laughed. 'Apparently, a long, long

time ago, there was a tooth fairy who taught at Glitterwings. I've read about how cosy she found it up there – so you see, Shadow had good reason to feel drawn to it!'

Twink thought of how prickly Shadow had seemed when they'd first met. She had a feeling that Shadow would be much happier now that she was back home again, teaching the other tooth fairies how to make carvings like she did!

Miss Shimmery squeezed her shoulder. 'Come along,' she said. 'Let's go and join your friends.'

Twink felt like singing as the cool evening breeze tickled her wings. Catching up with Bimi and Sooze, she smiled at them. 'Is everything all right?' whispered Bimi.

'Better than all right,' Twink whispered back.

Just ahead, she could see Glitterwings Academy, rising up from its hill in the moonlight. Her heart swelled. Oh, she was the luckiest fairy in the world! Not only did she go to the best school ever, but she had the most wonderful friends that anyone could have wished for.

'Look, Opposite,' said Sooze, nudging her with her wing. 'There's the branch that started it all.'

Twink smiled as she gazed at the tiny branch at the top of the tree. How funny to think that the only reason she'd gone up there in the first place was for her term project! She grinned at her friends, linking her arms tightly through theirs as they flew.

'Well, I definitely learned something new about Glitterwings, didn't I?' she laughed. 'I'm going to have the most glimmery report ever!'

To find out about other
glimmery Glitterwings
Academy stories,
turn over the page

Titania Woods

There are lots more stories about Glitterwings
Academy – make sure you haven't missed any of them!

If you have any difficulty in finding these in your local bookshop,
please visit www.bloomsbury.com or call 020 7440 2475
to order direct from Bloomsbury Publishing.

Visit www.glitterwingsacademy.co.uk for more fabulous fairy fun!